THE LITTLE MATCH GIRL
By Hans Christian Andersen
Translated from the original Danish text by Marlee Alex
Illustrated by Toril Marö Henrichsen
Published by Scandinavia Publishing House,
Nørregade 32, DK-1165 Copenhagen; Denmark
Text:© Copyright 1984 Scandinavia Publishing House
Artwork:© Copyright 1984 Toril Marö Henrichsen and
Scandinavia Publishing House
Printed in Italy

ISBN 0 8317-5548-2

The Little Match Girl

Hans Christian Andersen
Illustrated by Toril Marö Henrichsen

GALLERY BOOKS
An Imprint of W. H. Smith Publishers Inc.
112 Madison Avenue
New York City 10016

It was terribly cold. It was snowing and getting dark as evening approached. It was the last evening of the year, New Year's Eve. In the cold and darkness, a little girl walked along the street; a poor girl with a bare head and bare feet. She had had slippers on when she left home, but they were her mother's slippers and they were so big that the little girl had lost them when she hurried across the street to avoid being hit by two racing carriages. She could not find one of the slippers again, and a boy had run off with the other one.

The little girl's small feet were red and blue from the cold. In an old apron she carried some matchsticks and in her hand she held another bundle of them. No one had bought any from her that day, and no one had given her a penny. She was hungry, cold and sad; the poor little thing!

Snowflakes fell on her long, golden hair which curled beautifully around her shoulders. But she didn't care about how she looked. In all the windows candles were shining, and even in the street it smelled wonderfully of roast goose! It was New Year's Eve! That's what she was thinking about.

In a corner between two houses she sat down and huddled up. She pulled her small legs up under her but she grew even colder. She dared not go home for she hadn't sold any matchsticks; she hadn't earned a single penny and her father would beat her. Besides, it was just as cold at home for they had only a poor roof over their heads through which the wind blew, although the biggest cracks were stuffed with straw and rugs.

Her small hands were
almost completely numb with the cold.
Oh! A little matchstick might help, if only
she dared to pull one out of the bundle, strike it against
the wall and warm her fingers. Finally, she was so cold that she drew one out,
"ritsh!" How it sputtered, how it flickered! It was warm and bright like
a little candle. When she held her hand around
it it gave a strange light.

The little girl dreamt she was sitting in front of a large iron stove with shiny brass knobs and brass handles. The fire blazed gloriously and it warmed her so nicely. But, what was this? The little girl stretched out her feet to warm them as well, and the flame went out. The stove disappeared. She sat with the stub of the burnt out match in her hand.

She struck another one; it flickered and it flared up, and where it shone on the wall, the wall became transparent as a veil. She saw right into the parlour where the table was set with a shiny white cloth and fine dinnerware. Steam rose into the air from a roast goose stuffed with prunes and apples. And what was even more remarkable, the goose jumped down from the platter, and waddled across the floor with a knife and fork in its back. Right over to the poor little girl it came; then the flame went out and there was only the thick cold wall to see.

She struck another match
and found herself sitting under the
most beautiful Christmas tree. It
was larger and prettier
than the one she had seen through
the glass door of the rich merchant.
A thousand candles flickered
on its green branches, and coloured
pictures looked down at her. The
little girl reached out towards the
tree, and the match went out.
The candles rose higher and
higher into the sky. She saw
now that they were bright stars.
One of them fell and drew a long trail
of fire across the sky.

"Someone is dying now!"
said the little girl. Her old
grandmother, the only
person who had been good to
her but who was now dead,
had said that when a star fell, a
soul went up to God.
She struck another
matchstik against the wall. It
gave light around her, and in the
glimmer stood the old
woman; her grandmother, so
bright and radiant,
gentle and loving.

"Grandma!" shouted the little girl, "Oh, take me with you! I know you will disappear when the match goes out; disappear just like the stove, the lovely goose, and the big, wonderful Christmas tree!" And she quickly struck the last few matchsticks in the bundle, for she wanted to keep Grandmother within reach. The matches lit up with such a glow that they were brighter than daylight. Grandmother had never before been so beautiful, so strong; she lifted the little girl up in her arms, and they flew in glory and joy, so high, so high. And there was no cold, no hunger, no fear.

20

In the cold morning, the little girl sat
in the corner by the house, with
rosy cheeks and a smile on her lips,
dead; frozen to death on the last
evening of the old year. New Year's
morn rose over the little body which
was found with the burnt out
matchsticks. People said she had
tried to warm herself. None of them
knew what beautiful things she had
seen, nor how, with her old
grandmother, she had gloriously
entered into the New Year's joy.